D1541617

J
FIC
LON

Mullarkey, Lisa.
Jack London's White
    fang.

[67600]

PLEASE WASH
YOUR HANDS
BEFORE YOU READ ME
AND KEEP ME CLEAN

Demco

CALICO ILLUSTRATED CLASSICS

Jack London's

White Fang

ADAPTED BY: Lisa Mullarkey
ILLUSTRATED BY: Anthony VanArsdale

magic wagon

visit us at www.abdopublishing.com

Published by Magic Wagon, a division of the ABDO Group,
8000 West 78th Street, Edina, Minnesota 55439. Copyright
© 2011 by Abdo Consulting Group, Inc. International copyrights
reserved in all countries. All rights reserved. No part of this
book may be reproduced in any form without written permission
from the publisher.

Calico Chapter Books™ is a trademark and logo of Magic Wagon.

Printed in the United States of America, Melrose Park, Illinois.
102010
012011

 This book contains at least 10% recycled materials.

Original text by Jack London
Adapted by Lisa Mullarkey
Illustrated by Anthony VanArsdale
Edited by Stephanie Hedlund and Rochelle Baltzer
Cover and interior design by Abbey Fitzgerald

Library of Congress Cataloging-in-Publication Data

Mullarkey, Lisa.
  White Fang / Jack London ; adapted by Lisa Mullarkey ; illustrated
by Anthony VanArsdale.
     p. cm. -- (Calico illustrated classics)
   ISBN 978-1-61641-112-1
   [1. Dogs--Fiction. 2. Wolves--Fiction. 3. Human-animal
relationships--Fiction. 4. Yukon--History--19th century--Fiction.] I.
VanArsdale, Anthony, ill. II. London, Jack, 1876-1916. White Fang.
III. Title.
   PZ10.3.M8Wh 2011
   [Fic]--dc22
                                    2010031051

Table of Contents

The Trail of the Meat

The dark spruce forest frowned on both sides of the frozen waterway. The trees had been stripped of their snow by a biting wind. They now leaned toward each other in a black mass.

The land itself was deserted and lifeless. There was no movement. If you listened closely, there was a laughter that could be heard. Not a laughter of happiness. Rather, the evil laughter of the Wild.

But there *was* life in the land. Defiant life in the wolfish dogs near the waterway. Their fur was covered with frost. Their breath froze in the air as it left their mouths.

A leather harness was on the dogs, and leather traces attached to a sled that was dragged behind them. The sled was without runners. On the sled was a long, narrow box. Also found on top was an ax, blankets, a coffee pot, and a frying pan. But, occupying most of the space was the box.

In front of the dogs as well as in the back was a man. On the sled, in the box, lay a third man. A man whom the Wild had conquered. He was beaten down until he would never struggle or move again.

The Wild does not like movement. The Wild aims to destroy movement and life. It freezes the water to prevent its way to the sea. It drives the sap out of trees till they are frozen. And man? It destroys man to the core.

But, at the front and back of the sled worked two men who were not yet dead. Their bodies were covered in fur and soft-tanned leather. Their eyelashes, cheeks, and lips were so coated with crystals from their frozen breath that you could not tell who was who. They looked like ghosts. But underneath their white masks, two adventurers were pitting themselves against the Wild, determined to win.

They traveled on without speaking. Silence surrounded them on all sides. When the sun started to fade, a faint cry arose in the air. The front man turned his head until he locked eyes with the second. Then, across the narrow box, the two men nodded at each other.

A second cry pierced the silence. Both men turned to face the area they had just come from. A third, answering cry arose in the same spot.

"They're after us," said Bill to the man in the front. His voice was hoarse.

"Meat is scarce," answered his friend, Henry. "I ain't seen a rabbit for days."

Although they didn't speak again, each time they heard the cry, they gave a nodding look to each other.

At the fall of darkness, the men swung their dogs into a cluster of spruce trees and made camp. The coffin served as chair and table. The wolf dogs stayed on the other side of the

fire. Although they snarled and bickered, they made no attempt to stray into the darkness.

"Seems to me, Henry, that they're staying remarkably close to camp," said Bill.

Henry, squatting over the fire with the coffee pot, nodded. "They know their hides are safe. They'd sooner eat grub than be grub. They're pretty wise, them dogs."

Bill shook his head. "Oh, I don't know about that. Did you happen to notice the way the dogs kicked up while I was feeding them?"

"They did cut up more than the usual," replied Henry.

"How many dogs we got, Henry?"

"Six," said Henry.

"Well, Henry, I took six fish out of the bag. I gave one fish to each dog. But I was short, Henry. One fish short."

"You counted wrong, Bill."

"I didn't count wrong. One Ear didn't get a fish. I won't say they were all dogs, but there was seven lined up for fish."

"There's six now. Just counted them."

"I saw one run across the snow."

Henry sighed. "I'll be glad when this trip is done and over. I think it's getting to you, too. You're seeing things."

"I thought of that," said Bill. "But I counted them and saw the tracks of the one that ran off."

"Then you're thinking it was one of them?"

A long wailing cry, fiercely sad, from somewhere in the darkness interrupted them.

Bill pointed. "One of them, for sure."

Cry after cry could be heard from the distance. It shattered the silence and angered the Wild. The sled dogs huddled in fear by the fire. So close did they gather that their fur was singed by the flames. Looking out around the fire, a circle of eyes, like gleaming coals, could be seen getting closer.

"Wish we had more than three bullets left, Henry. I wish we had 300. I'd show them," said Bill. "And I wish this cold snap would break. Fifty below for over two weeks is frightful."

Henry settled into bed by the fire. "What's got me thinking is, why didn't the dogs pitch a fit when that other one ate a fish of theirs? Don't make sense."

Bill was already asleep. They slept side by side. As the fire died down, the circle of eyes drew closer. When they got too close for the dogs, they started an uproar.

Bill got up and added more wood to the fire, which kept the circles at bay. "Henry," said Bill, getting under the covers, "there are seven again. Just counted."

In the morning, Bill awoke first and made some coffee. "Say, Henry, how many dogs we got?"

"Six."

"Wrong, Henry."

"Seven again?" Henry asked.

"Wrong again. We got five. One's gone. It's Fatty. They ate him alive." He looked at the tracks. "Just dragged him off and ate him alive, I bet."

The She-Wolf

Night after night, a dog went missing. It was Kiche, who was part dog and part wolf, who led them to their death. She knew the way of the man-animals. Because she looked so much like a husky, Kiche was barely noticed standing among the others.

She was a daring beast. She would slink into camp and eat their food. But what little food they had wasn't enough for her or the pack she ran with. So each evening, she would enter the camp and lure a dog out into an open field.

She would trot up to them, touch noses, and play. When they trusted her, she led them away from camp. Once they were alone in a field, the pack would appear and pounce. Kiche did this until there were no dogs left.

Bill and Henry felt hopeless.

"We can't just sit here waiting to be eaten," said Bill. He grabbed his rifle. "I got three bullets left, and I plan to make good use of them. Those wolves are hungry. Their bellies need to be full, and I'm guessin' we're their next meal."

The men continued on their journey. About a mile away, they saw Kiche before them.

"Looks like a dog to me," said Bill. "I wouldn't be surprised if she started to wag her tail."

Henry agreed. "It does look like a dog. I ain't never seen a red wolf before. She's the color of cinnamon."

"Hello, husky!" cried Bill.

Kiche inched toward them.

"She ain't a bit afraid of us," said Bill. He pulled a rifle from the sled. When he held it up, Kiche ran off.

"Look at that," he said. "She's seen a rifle before. Smart wolf. Too smart to let me shoot her out here in the open. When the time is right, I'm going to kill her."

Bill had his chance the next day. "I see her tracks. I'm going to hunt her down."

Henry couldn't talk Bill out of it. Bill was determined to kill Kiche. It wasn't long before Henry heard a commotion of yelps, three shots, an even larger commotion, and then silence. The land was calm once more.

Henry found Bill, or what remained of him, hours later. That night, Henry knew he had little chance of surviving. The fire was low and the wolves were bolder than ever. As he rested his eyes, he shouted, "Come and get me 'cause I'm tired. You're going to win anyway." The last thing he saw was the red she-wolf circling his body.

When he woke up hours later, he sensed something had changed. He sat up and couldn't see the wolves. He didn't hear the wolves. The fire was still burning.

"Morning," came a voice. "If we didn't arrive when we did, you would have been the wolves' next meal."

Henry saw a musher throwing sticks on the fire. When he looked over his shoulder, he saw four sleds with half a dozen men crouched in front of another fire.

"Where's Lord Alfred?" asked one of the men.

"In a box," said Henry. "I wasn't going to let the wolves get him."

"And your partner?"

But Henry didn't need to answer. They knew.

Far and faint as it was, in the remote distance, the cry of a hungry wolf pack could be heard.

It was Kiche who first heard the approaching men. She led the wolves away from danger and led the front of the pack. Next to her was One Eye. He did not snarl at her, for he was quite taken with her. It was she who snarled at him when he got too close.

Their situation was desperate. They were hungry and growing weaker with each step. They ran slower than usual. The strongest, although still weak, ran at the front. Those near death stayed in the rear. As they ran, no life stirred. There was no food to have.

They ran many miles that day and through the night. At noon the next day, they crossed low divides and a dozen small streams before they were rewarded. They came upon a moose. He was meat and life. It was a good fight, but in the end, the moose was defeated. Kiche tore at his throat and devoured him alive.

The moose provided 800 pounds of food. The forty some dogs ate it all at one sitting.

There was now much rest and sleep. Soon after, the pack split in half. Kiche and One Eye led their half of the pack down to the Mackenzie River and across the lakes. The pack continued to dwindle until Kiche and One Eye were alone.

They kept together as the days passed by. They hunted and killed their meat together. They ate together. After a time, Kiche became restless. She seemed to be searching for something she couldn't find. The hallows under fallen trees seemed to attract her. She spent many hours poking and prodding. One Eye had no interest in such things and would sit and wait patiently.

They didn't remain in one place. They traveled quickly. One day, One Eye stopped suddenly. Kiche's ears rose. She darted to a clearing. One Ear cautiously approached her. Together, they stood watching, listening, and smelling.

They heard sounds of dogs wrangling and scuffling. Voices of scolding women and crying children could be heard. They smelled an array of scents from the Indian camp before them.

Kiche became increasingly excited. One Ear grew more cautious. His eyes told her he wanted to leave. She nuzzled his neck begging to stay. How she longed to move forward toward the fire, the people, and the dogs!

For two days, Kiche and One Eye hung about the camp. He didn't understand how such a place could call to his mate. But on the third morning, after a bullet hit the tree above One Eye's head, they fled.

They didn't go too far. Kiche once again appeared to be searching for something. Her running slowed, and she rested most of the day.

Finally, she found the thing she sought. It was a small cave. She rushed inside to investigate. Although the roof barely cleared her head, it was dry and cozy. With a small grunt, she dropped and curled up beside the wall.

One Eye rested outside at the mouth of the cave. He glanced at his mate, who showed no desire to move. The land was awakening and he

wanted to explore. He was about to go in search of food when he heard strange noises coming from the cave.

He approached Kiche and saw five cubs curled up beside her. The she-wolf snarled and showed her teeth to One Eye.

But One Eye posed no threat. He had heard that some fathers eat their newborns, but he had no such desire. Instead, he left the cave and went to get food for his family. His instincts told him that this is what he was meant to do.

One Eye returned to the mouth of the cave hours later. With a nervous walk, he entered and laid a porcupine by Kiche's feet. The she-wolf inspected it, turned her muzzle to him, and lightly licked his neck.

In the next instant, she was warning him to stay away from the cubs. Her snarl wasn't as harsh as before. After all, One Eye was behaving as a father should by providing food for his family.

The Gray Cub

The gray cub was different than his brothers and sisters. They had the hair of Kiche. But he took after his father. He had bred true to One Eye's wolf stock.

The gray cub's eyes had not been open long. Yet, already he could see with steady clearness. And while his eyes had still been closed, he had felt, tasted, and smelled. He knew his two brothers and two sisters well.

He was a fierce cub. By far, he was the fiercest and strongest of his litter. He made a louder raspy growl than the others. His rages were more terrible than theirs. And he certainly caused his mother the most trouble.

Only a month old, he now stayed awake for longer periods of time. He came to learn of his new world. It was a dark and gloomy world, but he didn't know it since it was the only world he knew. His world was small. The limits were the walls of the lair.

The gray cub quickly discovered that one wall was different from the others. This was the mouth of the cave and a source of light. He was attracted to the light like a plant to the sun. But he quickly learned that he was not to approach the light. When he did, his mother would slap her paw on his nose or turn the young cub over.

The light was strange. He couldn't understand why his father would walk toward the light then disappear. He accepted the disappearing wall without question for some time.

Like most animals in the Wild, he learned hunger. A great famine had come to the Wild. Not only did the meat supply stop, but so did the milk from his mother.

At first, the cubs whimpered and cried because of their empty bellies. Then, they slept. There were no more squabbles. No more tiny rages. No more attempts to go toward the light. The gray cub was the only one of his brothers and sisters to survive the famine.

One Eye had become desperate and often went to search for food. Kiche had to leave the lair to search as well.

Then came the day when the gray cub no longer saw his father appearing and disappearing in the wall. This had happened at the end of a second and less severe famine. Kiche knew why he didn't return. When she went searching for food, she saw what was left of One Eye. A lynx had engaged him in battle and won.

Kiche found the lair of the lynx but didn't dare go inside. There were babies inside. She knew that there was nothing the lynx wouldn't do to protect her young. It was the same for her.

But the Wild is the Wild. Motherhood is motherhood. For the sake of her young cub, she returned to him. She knew the time would come when she would revisit this lair and seek her revenge.

The hunting was up to Kiche now. She left the cave more often. It gave the gray cub more opportunities to explore the light.

As he approached the disappearing wall, the light became brighter. He was dazzled by it. He went to the edge of the light and looked down. The ground was not solid under him.

He gazed down and was surprised at the greenness he saw. Within seconds, he tumbled off of the small cliff and rolled down the hill. This was a new world to him. A scary world.

As scary as it was, it fascinated him. He inspected the grass beneath him, put his nose in a dead tree trunk, and saw his first squirrel. The squirrel gave him great a scare. But when he snarled, it ran up a tree. This boosted his confidence.

He soon came upon a bird's nest. At first he was frightened of the baby chicks. Once he realized that he was much bigger than them, he became bolder. He touched one with his paw. Then he sniffed one before putting it in his mouth. His instincts told him to chew. So he snapped his jaws shut. The food was very good. He didn't stop chewing until every last chick was eaten.

Proud of himself, he started back to the cave. But when he rose up from the nest, he was blinded by the rush of the mother bird's angry wings.

The bird was in a fury. This caused a fury to rise in the cub as well. It was his first battle. But neither won the battle. For as he was about to sink his fangs into the bird, a hawk swooped down and carried it off.

He was very afraid of this flying creature. It took him a long time to come out from the brush where he sought safety. When he finally felt bold enough, he crawled out only to be pounced upon by a weasel. The weasel knocked him off his feet as she buried her teeth into his neck.

The gray cub would have died if Kiche hadn't come bounding out of the bushes. Seconds later, the cub was free, enjoying another fine meal of meat.

His desire to kill grew stronger as the days passed. But famine once again came his way. He was now expected to hunt for his food, and he quickly realized how scarce food was.

The famine didn't last long and was officially over when his mother returned one day. She dropped a lynx kitten in front of him. It was all for him! What he didn't know was that she had eaten the others all by herself.

As the two rested after their meal, a strange noise could be heard at the mouth of the cave. It was the mother lynx! The lynx was angry that her babies were taken from her. Although she could not leap inside, she crawled on her belly into the mouth and was immediately attacked by the two wolves. Kiche's revenge was complete.

After that, the gray cub accompanied his mother on the meat trail. He understood his part in the killings. It was then that he learned the law of meat.

There were two kinds of meat. His own kind and the other kind. His own kind included his mother and himself.

The other kind was anything that was alive and moved. But the other kind was divided. One part was composed of non-killers and small killers. The other portion killed and ate his own kind or was eaten by his own kind. This is how the law came about: eat or be eaten.

He preferred to eat.

Life was once again good. He was very much alive, happy, and proud of himself.

CHAPTER 4

The Makers of Fire

The cub was in the habit of awaking from sleep and running on a familiar trail down to the stream to drink. He had traveled on the trail often. It was always the same. This time, however, the smells were different as he trotted among the trees.

Then, in an instant, he saw what he smelled. Before him, sitting quietly, were five live things. Things he had never seen before. It was his first glimpse of mankind.

The five men did not rise, show teeth, or snarl. They didn't move. Nor did the cub move.

Every instinct was telling him to dash away. But a new instinct rose within that compelled him to stay. It was awe. Something told him that these were powerful creatures. More powerful than anything he had encountered so far.

One of the Indians rose and walked over to the cub. As the man reached down to grab him, the cub cowered and showed his fangs. The Indian laughed.

"Wabam wabisca ip pit tah," (Look! The white fangs!) he said.

The other men laughed and urged the man to pick up the cub. As the man's hands approached

him, the cub's natural instincts took over. In a snap, the white fangs sank into the Indian's hand.

Within seconds, the man smacked the cub in his head. His blow knocked the cub over to his side. In an instant, the instinct to fight faded as he sat up on his legs and yelped.

The Indian was angry. He kicked the cub once more. A loud yelping filled the air.

The four Indians laughed again. Even the man bitten laughed. The cub was hurt and continued to cry. In the midst of his tears, the cub heard something. The Indians must have heard it as well for they stood back.

It was Kiche coming to the rescue of her cub! She bounded in amongst them as the men moved farther back. The she-wolf stood over her cub, snarling a deep rumble in her throat.

Then a cry went up from one of the men. "Kiche!"

The cub felt his mother's stance soften. At once, her tail wagged.

The cub didn't understand. He was confused by his mother's behavior. Did she know the powers of these men?

The man who yelled Kiche's name came over and patted her head. The others did the same. Kiche didn't snap or threaten to snap. She wagged her tail faster.

"Kiche's mother was my brother's dog," explained Gray Beaver. "She mated with a wolf years ago and Kiche was the result. A year ago, she ran away due to the famine. She must have mated with a wolf since then." He reached out to touch the cub. "This cub is the result."

The cub snarled and sank his fangs into the hand once again. Gray Beaver laughed. "Yes, Kiche is his mother. But his father was a wolf. Within him, there is little dog but much wolf. Since his fangs are white, he shall be called White Fang. I have spoken. He is my dog now for Kiche was my brother's dog. And now, my brother is dead."

White Fang was tired. He lay down and watched as Gray Beaver took his knife and cut a branch off a tree. He fastened strings of rawhide to each end. He tied one string around Kiche's throat and the other around a small tree. White Fang curled up next to his mother.

Gray Beaver rolled White Fang onto his back and playfully rubbed his stomach. Although this frightened White Fang at first, he came to enjoy the feeling.

After a time, White Fang heard strange noises approaching. A few minutes later, the rest of the tribe marched into camp. Men, women, children, and dogs came quickly.

White Fang had never seen dogs before. Seeing them, he knew at once that they were like him in many ways but also a bit different. He soon learned they were unfriendly as they rushed toward him, snapping their jaws and slashing him with their teeth.

Kiche did her best to protect her cub, but she couldn't reach White Fang. She was tied to the tree. It wasn't until the man-animals fought the dogs back with club blows that White Fang was safe once again. He knew these men were powerful. They set the laws and did what they must to make sure they were obeyed by the dogs. They had godlike power.

White Fang licked his wounds for a short time before they were led on a new adventure. Led by Gray Beaver's son, Mit-sah, they walked to the river.

White Fang couldn't stop looking at the poles in the ground that had strange cloths and skins on them. Their sheer size surprised him. He was afraid of these teepees. But as soon as he saw children passing in and out of them without harm, his fear passed.

After some time, White Fang wandered away from Kiche and headed toward a teepee. He approached carefully and sniffed the cloth. He waited. Nothing happened. He closed his teeth on the strange fabric and gently pulled. Nothing happened. He tugged harder and harder until the entire teepee collapsed. The sharp cry of the squaw inside sent him scampering back to his mother for safety.

He was growing braver by the minute and soon left the safety of his mother's side again. This time, it was to approach a small puppy named Lip-lip.

Lip-lip was White Fang's own kind. Seeing this, White Fang greeted him in a playful manner. But Lip-lip showed his teeth and, within seconds, pounced on White Fang. He shredded White Fang's shoulder with his teeth. It was the first of many fights these two would have.

White Fang jumped back in pain and ran to his mother. It was there that he learned to stay away from Lip-lip, who was known as a bully about camp. Kiche licked her cub's wounds and soothed him.

Soon, White Fang wanted to explore once again. He saw Gray Beaver squatting and holding sticks and dry moss on the ground. He watched as Gray Beaver accepted twigs and sticks from the Indian children. Minutes later, as White Fang sat by Gray Beaver's knee, he saw a strange mist rise from the sticks and moss. The color of the sky's sun was now on the sticks!

White Fang knew nothing of fire. He was drawn to it just like the light had called to him during his early days in the cave. He crawled toward the fire. He was so close, his nose touched the flame at the same time his little tongue reached out to it.

For a moment, he was paralyzed. Then, he yelped cries of pain. He had never known such pain before. Hearing her cub's cries, Kiche tried to break free from the tree.

Gray Beaver laughed and slapped his thighs. He told anyone who would listen what the silly cub did. White Fang tried to soothe his burned nose, but his tongue had been hurt too. As he desperately tried to reach his mother for help, he was surrounded by more men and children laughing.

White Fang now knew shame. The fire had hurt him, but the man-animals' laughter hurt much more.

As nighttime came, White Fang grew more and more homesick. This land was too noisy. The men were too powerful. The bickering between dogs never ended. The hum never stopped.

He watched as the men rushed back and forth and knew they were superior creatures. They could make fire. They could force animals to obey with sticks. They were fire makers. They were gods!

CHAPTER 5

The Way of the Wild

As time passed, White Fang grew to respect these man-gods more and more. When they walked, he got out of their way. When they called, he came. When they threatened, he cowered down. When they commanded him to go, he rushed away. He belonged to them as all dogs belonged to them. His actions were theirs to command.

While he knew he must stay with them, there were days he longed to run free in the Wild. Those instincts would never fade. Although he had opportunities to run into the Wild, it was the thought of his mother that held him back.

White Fang came to understand the camp. He knew the greediness of the older dogs when meat or fish was thrown out to be eaten. He

came to know that men were more just, children more cruel, and women more kindly. He also learned to stay away from mothers of puppies, for they would do anything to protect their young.

He also knew that Lip-lip, who was bigger, older, and stronger, despised him. He picked White Fang as his enemy. Lip-lip proved to be a nightmare for White Fang. Whenever he ventured away from his mother, Lip-lip would appear and attack him. Lip-lip always won the battle and took great delight in doing so.

With each defeat, White Fang grew more vicious and angry. The playful side of him disappeared as Lip-lip refused to allow any puppies to play with him.

Anytime White Fang would approach a dog for friendship, Lip-lip would force them away. He robbed White Fang of his puppyhood ,which only made White Fang more determined to get revenge.

One day, White Fang got his first taste of revenge. White Fang was a fast runner, but on this day he allowed Lip-lip to stay close and chase him about the camp. He barely stayed one step in front of Lip-lip.

Lip-lip enjoyed the chase and forgot where he was. When he remembered, it was too late. He was already in Kiche's punishing jaws. For White Fang had led him to her!

Kiche repeatedly ripped and slashed Lip-lip with her fangs. White Fang joined in and gnashed at his legs. By the time they finished their assault, Lip-lip crawled away barely able to walk.

Soon after, Gray Beaver rewarded Kiche with her freedom. He no longer felt she would run away. He freed her from the leash. Kiche and White Fang spent the day exploring the camp and the world beyond it.

When White Fang tried to move farther into the woods, Kiche wouldn't go. She turned to look back at the camp. White Fang tried to nudge her forward, but she refused to move. Reluctantly, he joined her as she returned to camp.

There was something calling him out there in the open. His mother heard it, too. But she heard another, louder call. The call of fire and man. That call, for Kiche, was stronger than the restraints placed upon her at camp. For now, White Fang needed his mother more than he needed the Wild.

The Indians didn't care that White Fang needed his mother. Gray Beaver had a debt to repay to Three Eagles. Three Eagles needed to travel down the Mackenzie River. Gray Beaver repaid his debt with Kiche.

As Kiche was taken on Three Eagles's canoe, White Fang tried to follow her. As he leaped into the canoe, a club forced him into the water. The canoe shoved off with White Fang swimming behind it. He blocked out the cries of Gray Beaver to return to shore at once.

This enraged Gray Beaver. He shoved off in his own canoe and overtook White Fang. Grabbing him by the nape of the neck, he lifted White Fang out of the water. He didn't drop him into the canoe. Instead, Gray Beaver held him high with one hand while beating him with his other hand.

White Fang had never received such a beating. Finally, he showed his teeth and attempted to bite Gray Beaver. This only made Gray Beaver angrier and the blows more forceful.

After White Fang's yelps reached a fevered pitch, Gray Beaver dropped him to the floor of the canoe. When they reached shore, Gray Beaver threw him to the ground. Having witnessed all of it, Lip-lip pounced on White Fang and planned on finishing him off. White Fang was too weak to defend himself.

To White Fang's surprise, it was Gray Beaver who came to his defense. He lifted Lip-lip over his head and flung him through the air. He crashed down upon the ground ten feet away.

The force was violent. White Fang knew that the right to punish was reserved for the gods only. It was denied to lesser creatures under them. Lip-lip had been foolish.

Although White Fang continued to search and mourn the loss of his mother, his loyalty toward Gray Beaver grew stronger. By obeying him, he got extra meat and protection from Lip-lip.

The fights with Lip-lip continued, but White Fang was growing stronger and more cunning. When the dogs ganged up on him, he would lead one out of the pack, just as his mother had done before him. He would shred the dog to pieces before the rest of the pack caught up.

It was the way of the Wild.

CHAPTER
6

The Outcast

Lip-lip continued to darken White Fang's days. This caused him to become even more wicked and ferocious. Savageness was part of his makeup, but his savageness exceeded his makeup.

His reputation among the animals was known among the Indians themselves. Whenever an uproar or trouble brewed in camp, White Fang was connected to the crime. He was a sneak and a thief. A mischiefmaker.

He found himself an outcast in camp. All the young dogs followed Lip-lip's lead. Out of the frequent attacks he learned two things. He knew how to take care of himself when several dogs attacked at once. And as a single dog, he learned how he could inflict the greatest amount of damage in the shortest amount of time.

White Fang became catlike in his ability to stay on his feet. If knocked off his feet, he knew death was possible. He learned the value of surprise and always strived to take the dogs off guard.

White Fang's method was an easy one. He would first find a dog alone. Then, he'd surprise it and knock it to the ground. Finally, he'd drive his teeth into its soft throat.

Many a dog walked around camp with scars from White Fang. He was hated around camp. Every tooth was out for him as well as the hand of every man.

The Wild had taught him a code: to obey the strong and to oppress the weak. Gray Beaver was a god. Therefore, White Fang obeyed him. But the dogs younger or smaller than himself were weak and things to be destroyed.

In order to become stronger, White Fang worked harder. He became quicker, swifter, crueler, and more ferocious than all the other dogs. If he hadn't, he would never have survived in the hostile environment in which he found himself.

In the fall of that year, White Fang got his chance for freedom. For several days, there had been a great hubbub in the village. The summer camp was being dismantled. The tribe was preparing to go off for the fall hunt.

White Fang watched it all with eager eyes. When the teepees came down, he understood.

He was determined to stay behind. He waited for his opportunity to slink into the woods. Then, he crawled through the dense thicket and waited until every canoe had departed.

Soon, White Fang could hear Gray Beaver calling his name. He saw Mit-sah and the squaw taking part in a search for him. He resisted the impulse to crawl out of hiding.

The voices died away as the evening grew dark. He stepped out bravely at first, but his bravery soon gave way to loneliness. And it was cold. There were no warm teepees to snuggle in. His stomach longed for meat, but there was none before him.

Noises of the wild invaded his ears and frightened him. A panic seized him. He made a mad dash in the direction of the village, but he had forgotten the village had been packed up and moved.

He rushed to where Gray Beaver's teepee had stood. He sat and pointed his nose at the moon. A sad cry bubbled from his throat. His grief for Kiche, his past sorrows, and the dangers of those to come, gripped him. It was a lone wolf howl, full throated and mournful. The first howl he ever uttered.

With daylight, White Fang's bravery returned. He ran without resting to the river, looking for the trail that the gods might have taken. By the second day, he had run for thirty hours straight and was weary. He was weak with hunger. His handsome coat was mangled. The broad pads of his feet were bruised and bleeding. He had begun to limp and, to make matters worse, the snow fell.

Luck was with White Fang. For Gray Beaver had brought down a moose on the bank of the river. If he had not, the Indians would have crossed the river. That would have been the end of White Fang. But White Fang smelled the food cooking and followed his nose to the camp.

He first saw the blaze of the fire. Then, he spotted Gray Beaver squatting and eating. White Fang approached cautiously, expecting a beating.

He crouched and bristled at the thought of it. At once, Gray Beaver heard White Fang.

There was movement of a hand above White Fang. He prepared himself for a beating but it never came. Instead, Gray Beaver's hand lowered and offered him meat.

Gray Beaver then ordered more meat and stood guard over White Fang as he ate it. No dogs would be allowed to steal from him that evening. White Fang dozed by the fire. He was content knowing that he was in camp with the man-animals, the gods to whom he had given himself and was now dependent upon.

CHAPTER 7

The Laws of the Gods

In December, Gray Beaver took his family on a journey up the Mackenzie River. It was time to teach Mit-sah how to drive a dog team. It was perfect timing since the new puppies themselves had to be broken into the harness.

There were seven puppies on the team. The others were nine and ten months old while White Fang, the youngest, was eight months old.

Each dog was fastened to the sled by a different length of rope. This way, they could fan out and not run into the dog ahead of him. White Fang welcomed this, as he had seen many dogs do this at camp.

The journey continued for many months. White Fang was happy pulling Mit-sah's sled.

He learned many things from Gray Beaver and Mit-sah on this trip.

Long ago, Gray Beaver had taught him that it was a crime to bite one of the gods. But as White Fang arrived in the village at Great Slave Lake, his views on the law changed. There were times when it was acceptable to bite a man-god!

In this village, dogs were allowed to search for food. On White Fang's first search, he came upon a boy chopping frozen moose meat with an ax. Chips flew into the air and landed at White Fang's feet. He ate the chips. When the boy saw this, he started to chase White Fang with a club. White Fang fled between two teepees and was trapped. There was no escape.

White Fang was furious at the boy who held the club above his head! He faced the boy and snarled. He knew the laws of foraging. All meat on the ground was for dogs. He had done no wrong. Broken no law. Yet, this boy was preparing to punish him. Out of rage, White Fang attacked the boy and ripped his hand open.

White Fang knew he had broken the law of the gods. He had driven his teeth into one of them! He expected a fierce punishment. He fled toward Gray Beaver and was surprised to find Gray Beaver defend him. So did Mit-sah. They knew White Fang's attack was justified.

This is when he learned that there were different gods. His gods and other gods. There was a difference between the two. Justice or injustice, it was all the same. He had to take

both from his gods, but injustice from the other gods was not tolerated.

Before the day ended, White Fang learned more about this law. He was in the woods with Mit-sah when they came upon the boy White Fang had bitten. Other boys were there, too. They attacked Gray Beaver's son. Blows fell on him from all sides. White Fang looked on at first. For wasn't this an affair between two gods? It was no concern of his.

Then he realized it was one of his gods who was being mistreated. *His* god. A mad rush ran through his body as he leaped toward the crowd of boys. Five minutes later, the landscape was filled with fleeing boys. Many dripped with blood thanks to White Fang's teeth.

When Mit-sah told the story in camp, Gray Beaver ordered meat for White Fang. Another twist to the law. Protect your own. This law was the law of reward for protecting the man-god's family.

In the third year of White Fang's life, there came a great famine to the Mackenzie Indians. Fish and moose were scarce. The rabbits seemed to have disappeared. Hunting and preying animals perished. Felled by hunger, they started to devour each other.

There was wailing in the village as the women and children did without so the hunters could get the energy needed for hunting. The gods were driven to eat the soft tanned leather from their moccasins and mittens.

The dogs ate one another, and finally the gods ate the weakest dogs. The wisest of the dogs fled to the forest. In the end, those dogs starved or were eaten by wolves.

White Fang was wise and rushed into the woods. He was better suited to the woods than the other dogs. He had his cubhood to guide him. He was especially good at catching small things. Although he could catch squirrels with ease, there simply weren't enough of them to fill him.

When food was too scarce, he ran back to the village and stole what little food he could find there. Fortune seemed to favor him. Just when all hope would fade, he would find food, whether it was the remains of a kill or the discovery of a lone rabbit.

In the last days of the famine, White Fang had met up with Lip-lip, who had also escaped into the woods. Lip-lip had lived a miserable existence since leaving the village. They stared at each other face-to-face.

White Fang was in splendid condition. His hunting had been good and he had eaten his fill. As soon as he saw Lip-lip, the memories of constant bullying rushed over him. Lip-lip, weak and frail, was no match for White Fang.

White Fang wasted no time. He snarled and struck Lip-lip hard and forced him on his back. White Fang drove his teeth into Lip-lip's scrawny throat. There wasn't much of a fight as White Fang quickly put an end to his life.

Not long after, White Fang came to the edge of the forest. He saw a village below where the land had been empty just days before. Familiar scents, sights, and sounds came to him. It was the old village in a new place! The sounds were different. Gone were whimpers and wails.

The air was filled with the smell of fresh fish. White Fish rushed boldly out of the forest and trotted up to Gray Beaver's teepee. Gray Beaver was not there, but Kloo-kooch welcomed him with glad cries. White Fang laid down and waited for Gray Beaver's return.

CHAPTER
8

The Enemy of His Kind

When White Fang was five, he arrived at Fort Yukon with Gray Beaver. A whisper of the gold rush had reached Gray Beaver's ears. He had come with mittens and moccasins to trade. He would not have taken such a long trip if he didn't think his profits would be great. He had hoped for 100 percent profit, but what he got was 1,000 percent profit!

It was at Fort Yukon that White Fang saw his first white men. He quickly realized they were gods, too. Gods that were stronger than his Indian gods. They had bigger places where they rested and their boats were larger.

White Fang was curious to observe them and went about watching them from a safe distance.

When he saw no harm come to the dogs near them, he slowly approached the white men.

White Fang was a great curiosity to these men. His wolfish appearance caught their attention. They pointed him out to one another. This put White Fang on guard. When they tried to approach him, he showed his teeth until they backed away.

He quickly realized that there were many of these white gods. Every few days, a steamer would drop off men and take others away. He was curious as to why they came and went so frequently.

As much as the white gods impressed him, their dogs did not. They were of all shapes and sizes. They had hair to keep them warm instead of fur. None of them knew how to fight. That didn't stop White Fang and his instincts.

He would strike the dogs and cause harm. But he was wise. He knew that all gods, no matter what color, did not like to see their dogs harmed. So, he would attack and back away.

The rest of the Indian dogs would move in for the final kill.

It was after such a death that White Fang learned just how powerful the white men could be. After a man saw his dog torn to pieces, he withdrew a revolver and fired six times. Six of the pack lay dead or dying. What powerful tools these white gods had!

White Fang continued his fights and the dogs continued to be killed. White Fang didn't care. He felt no loyalty to them. It was a sport to him and a sport to the men who walked off of the steamer. Each time a new steamer arrived, the gods would make their way to see White Fang in battle. All knew of his savage ways.

While all the gods enjoyed watching White Fang in combat, no one enjoyed it more than Beauty Smith. This god was anything but a beauty! Nature had not been kind to him.

Smith was a small man with a tiny head. It was an odd shape. So much so that he was given the nickname Pinhead when he was a child. His eyes were large and far apart from each other. His jaw was enormous and it seemed to rest on his chest. His teeth were yellow and crooked.

Smith was known as a coward. He cooked for the men. Because of that, he was tolerated by all. But he was also feared, as he tended to rage on from time to time. The men worried he'd poison their food.

Smith was mesmerized by White Fang and would often approach him. White Fang wanted nothing to do with this man. He'd snarl, growl, and flash his teeth whenever Smith approached him. This would make the man back off. White Fang sensed he was evil. He hated the man.

Smith wanted White Fang. He offered Gray Beaver a large sum of money, but Gray Beaver would not sell him. Gray Beaver knew how valuable White Fang was and assured Smith that he'd never sell him.

But Beauty Smith was conniving. He continued to visit Gray Beaver's camp often.

When he visited, he would bring whiskey and offer some to Gray Beaver.

Soon, Gray Beaver had a strong thirst for the whiskey and would do anything to get it. He started to give his earnings to Smith for a bottle of whiskey. Soon, all his profits were lost. The only thing he had left to sell was White Fang, and that's exactly what he did.

At camp one evening, Gray Beaver was given a bottle of whiskey for White Fang. He tied a leather thong around White Fang's neck and handed him over to Beauty Smith.

When White Fang realized what was happening, he snapped his jaws down upon Smith's hands. Smith could not be stopped. He grabbed a club and brought it down on White Fang's head.

White Fang knew he could not win this battle. At least for now. He was led away and tied to a fence at Smith's house. Sometime during the night, White Fang bit the thong and cut it in two. He ran all the way back to Gray Beaver. It was where he belonged.

But the next morning, Gray Beaver took White Fang back to Beauty Smith's camp. Smith beat White Fang ten times worse than before.

White Fang knew he had broken the law. He was to obey his god no matter who it was. But White Fang didn't care about the law. Once again, he escaped to find his way back to his Indian-god.

Gray Beaver betrayed him once more and returned him to his new owner. This time the beating was so severe, it almost killed White Fang. There were no more attempts to escape. White Fang knew his fate.

If he had tried to run away, he wouldn't have found Gray Beaver anyway. For Gray Beaver had left to go back to his village, leaving White Fang with a new owner who was mad. A mad god who still had to be obeyed.

CHAPTER 9

The Reign of Terror

Under the strong arm of Beauty Smith, White Fang became a mad fiend. He was kept chained in a pen at the rear of the fort. It was there that Smith would tease and torment him.

The man quickly discovered the shame laughing caused White Fang, so he would be sure to laugh at him every chance he got. This caused White Fang to become even madder.

White Fang became filled with hate. Hate for these gods, hate for the chain around his neck, hate for the pen that confined him. He hated the very wood that made up the pen.

Most of all, he hated Beauty Smith.

But Smith had a purpose for tormenting White Fang. One day, a number of men gathered in the pen. Smith entered the pen with a club and unchained White Fang. Then, he hurried back out.

A minute later, the door to the pen opened again. White Fang was confused. Something unusual was happening.

The door opened wider as a huge dog was thrust inside. Then, the door slammed shut once again. White Fang had never seen such a dog! It was a mastiff. The sheer size didn't deter him, though. It was something that he could take his hate out on.

White Fang jumped in with a flash of his fangs and ripped open the mastiff's neck. Within a minute, the mastiff was dead.

The men cheered and applauded while Smith gloated and collected his money.

In the weeks that followed, White Fang defeated every dog that was sent into his pen. Smith started to bring two, three, and four dogs in at a time. Even outnumbered, they were no match for White Fang. He earned his nickname as the Fighting Wolf.

In the fall, Smith took White Fang up the Yukon to Dawson. When they arrived, men surrounded White Fang's cage. He was a legend known to all. Smith charged the men fifty cents just to look at White Fang.

White Fang was given no rest. If he lied down to rest, a sharp stick would jab his side to awaken him. He was taken out of his cage from time to time when a fight could be arranged a few miles from town. He never knew defeat.

As time went by, he had fewer fights. Men knew their dogs couldn't win, so Smith was compelled to pit wolves against him. These wolves were trapped by the Indians for the sole purpose of fighting White Fang. These fights always drew a crowd and Smith would make large sums of money from them.

Once a lynx was brought in. All who saw the lynx pounce on White Fang thought it was the end of him. But it wasn't.

After the defeat of the lynx, the fighting stopped for a while. That is until Tim Keenan arrived in town. With him came the first bulldog that had ever entered the Klondike. It was inevitable that this dog and White Fang would be brought together.

The day these two animals would fight arrived. Smith entered the pen and slipped the chain from White Fang's neck. He stepped back.

For once, White Fang did not immediately attack. He stood still, ears pricked forward, alert and curious. He had never seen such a strange looking dog!

Keenan shoved the bulldog forward. "Go to it." The animal waddled toward the center of the circle. He was short and squat. He came to a stop in front of White Fang and blinked.

"Go get him, Cherokee!" came cries from the crowd. "Eat him up!"

But Cherokee didn't seem too eager to fight. He wagged his tail.

Keenan stepped in and bent over his dog. He rubbed his body against the grain of the hair and made slight pushing movements. This seemed to irritate Cherokee. He started to growl.

The growls made the hair on White Fang's neck rise. Cherokee rushed forward in a swift run. With the same catlike moves, White Fang lashed out and ripped the bulldog's thick neck.

The bulldog didn't yelp. He simply followed White Fang around the pen. White Fang lashed out and struck Cherokee again. Once more,

the dog merely wagged his tail and followed White Fang.

This puzzled White Fang. Never had he seen such a dog. It had no hair protection, bled easily, and was soft all over.

Cherokee was puzzled by White Fang as well. He had never come across a dog that stayed his distance.

White Fang soon realized he couldn't get the soft underside of the throat. The bulldog stood too short. Its massive jaws added protection.

As time passed, White Fang continued to inflict damage to Cherokee and continued to dodge his attacks. The bulldog still followed him around.

Time and again, White Fang tried to knock Cherokee off his feet. But the difference in their height was too great. He tried to strike one too many times. He finally sailed over Cherokee and fell to the ground.

A gasp could be heard. The men had never seen White Fang lose his footing. In the next instant, White Fang was back on his feet, but not before Cherokee's jaws clamped down on his neck.

White Fang shook violently and tried to throw the bulldog off of him but had no luck. Round and round White Fang went, abandoning all reasoning. No matter how hard he tried to shake the fifty pounds off of him, he couldn't.

Cherokee was delighted with his grip and even enjoyed the frantic way White Fang moved through the air.

The only thing that stopped the frantic movements was exhaustion. White Fang lay down and tried to think of his next move. The bulldog was determined to get White Fang on his back. It only took him a minute before he succeeded in doing so. As he did, his chewing jaws worked faster and faster.

White Fang was having trouble breathing. It looked as if the battle was over. Had he lost his first fight?

Death Is Near

Beauty Smith did not want to lose money on this fight. He was angry. He took a step into the ring and pointed his finger at White Fang. Then, he began to tease White Fang and laugh at him.

Smith's planned worked. It threw White Fang into a rage. He stood once more, with the bulldog's teeth still in his neck. The teeth inched toward his jugular vein.

White Fang tried to shake him off but only fell once more. No matter how hard he tried to rise again, he had no strength to do so.

Shouts went up. "Cherokee, Cherokee!" The dog wagged his tail. Smith kicked White Fang. "Get up, you beast. You lazy beast!"

White Fang did not move.

In the distance came a jingling of bells. The sound drew closer. Dog mushers!

The mushers stopped their dogs and joined the crowd. They were curious as to what the fuss was all about.

It was then that they saw an enraged Smith kicking White Fang. The tall musher broke through the crowd and smashed a blow on Smith's face.

"Cowards! All of you," he said as he faced the crowd. "You beasts!" He was in a rage himself.

Smith stood up and walked toward the man. The man lifted his hands again and smashed him over backward with a second blow.

"You beast," he repeated. He called to his friend, "Come help me, Matt. Lend a hand."

Both men bent over the dogs. Matt took hold of White Fang and was ready to pull when Cherokee's jaw tightened. As hard as they tried, neither could loosen the grip.

"It's no use, Mr. Scott. You can't break them apart," Matt said at last.

The pair paused to survey the dogs. "We ain't got much time," said Matt. "He's closing in on the jugular."

Cherokee wagged his tail while maintaining the grip. His eyes never left his master.

"Won't some of you help?" yelled Mr. Scott. "We need help."

No one came forward. Matt reached for his revolver. "You'll have to pry his mouth open with this." He tried to thrust its muzzle between the dog's jaws.

Keenan strode into the ring. "Don't be breaking any teeth. You break those teeth and there will be trouble—more trouble than you'll be wantin'."

"Then I'll have to break his neck," said Scott. He stared at the man. "Is this your dog?"

The man grunted. He nodded.

"Then break his grip," commanded Weedon Scott. "Do it now."

Keenan stood back and didn't reply. Finally, Matt accomplished what he had set out to do with the muzzle. The jaws were released.

Once the dogs were free, Keenan was ordered to carry his dog away. Now the men turned their attention toward White Fang. His eyes were half closed. Matt approached him and listened.

"He's still breathing, Mr. Scott."

Smith walked toward the dog.

"Matt, how much is a good sled dog worth?" asked Scott.

The dog musher thought for a moment. "Three hundred dollars."

Scott scratched his head. "And how much for one that's all chewed up like this one?"

"Half of that," was the answer.

"Did you hear, Mr. Beast?" asked Scott. "I'm taking your dog from you. I'm giving you $150 for him." He opened his bag and started to count out the bills.

Smith put his hands behind his back refusing to touch the money. "I ain't sellin' him."

"Oh, yes you are," said Scott. "You have no choice." He sprang toward Smith.

"I've got my rights," said Smith as he cowered. "You can't take my rights away from me."

"You gave up those rights," said Scott. He stood there with the money in his clenched fist. "Are you taking the money, or do I have to slug you again?"

"Oh, all right," sighed Smith. "But he's worth a mint. A man's got rights, you know."

"Correct," said Scott, passing the money to him. "But you're not a man. You're a beast, plain and simple. You got no rights."

"Wait till I get back to Dawson," threatened Smith. "I'll have the law on you. Both of you!"

"You do that," said Scott, "and I promise you that I'll run you out of every town you step foot in."

With that, he turned his attention to White Fang. And Scott, a man of great importance, meant every word he said.

CHAPTER 11

A Show of Kindness

"It's hopeless," Weedon Scott confessed. He sat on the step of his cabin and stared at the dog musher. "Not much we can do."

"Yep, hopeless," Matt agreed.

Together they looked at White Fang at the end of his chain. He was snarling and straining to get at the sled dogs.

"It's a wild one and there's no taming it," Scott announced.

"Oh, I don't know about that," said Matt. "Might be a lot of dog in him for all you can tell. But there's one thing I know for sure. Wolf or dog, he's been tamed already. I'm sure of it."

Scott didn't believe it.

"It's true," said Matt. "Look at those marks across his chest. He's had a harness on him."

Scott was surprised. "You're right, Matt. Must have been a sled dog before Smith got ahold of him. Think he can be a sled dog again?" he asked eagerly. Then he shook his head. "We've had him two weeks already. If anything, he's wilder than ever."

"Give him a chance and turn him loose for a bit," said Matt. "You tried before but did it without a club."

"You try it then," said Scott.

Matt grabbed a club and approached White Fang.

"Look at him keeping his eye on that club," said Matt. "That's a good sign. He's no fool." Matt unhooked the chain from White Fang's collar and stood back.

White Fang couldn't believe he was free! Many months had passed by since he was passed on to Smith. In all that time, he had never known freedom. He didn't know what to make of it.

He walked slowly and cautiously, never taking his eyes off of the white gods. He walked

quietly to the corner of the cabin and waited. Nothing happened.

"Won't he run away?" Scott asked. "He might take off any minute."

Matt shrugged his shoulders. "Got to take a gamble. Only way to find out is to find out."

"Poor devil," Scott muttered. "What he needs is some show of human kindness."

He reached into a bucket and pulled out a piece of meat. He tossed it to White Fang.

White Fang sprang away from it and studied it from a distance. Another dog, Major, made a dash for the meat. As his jaws clamped down on it, White Fang struck. Before Matt could step in, the snow was covered with Major's blood.

"That's too bad, but it served him right," said Scott.

Matt's foot was already in midair to kick White Fang. White Fang sprang into action and tore at Matt's leg.

Matt let out a cry of pain. "He got me all right," said Matt, examining his leg.

Scott withdrew his revolver. "We have no choice. It's the right thing to do."

Matt objected. "Look here, Mr. Scott. That dog's been through the toughest of times. Let's give him time." He rubbed his leg. "Serves me right. I had no right to kick him. I would have bit me, too."

"He's untamable," insisted Scott. "No way can we tame an animal like that."

Matt protested. "No one's given him a chance yet. We just turned him loose."

"God knows I don't want to kill him," said Scott. He put the gun away. "Let's let him run loose and see if kindness can work for him." He walked over to White Fang and began talking to him in a soothing way.

"Better have a club ready," warned Matt. "Don't get too close without one."

Scott shook his head and went on trying to win White Fang's confidence.

White Fang was suspicious. He waited for a beating. After all, he had just killed this god's dog and bitten the other god's leg. He was confused as to why this man carried no club. He didn't trust him.

Scott's hand drew closer. White Fang crouched and showed his teeth. Although Scott was quick to withdraw his hand, White Fang was quicker. His jaws snapped and Scott fell backward holding his torn hand.

White Fang bristled and backed away. Surely now he would be beaten.

Matt rushed into the cabin and came back with a rifle. "This has got to be done."

Just as Matt had pleaded for White Fang's safety when he was bitten, now it was Scott's time to beg for mercy.

"You said to give him a chance. Let's give it to him. We can't quit yet," said Scott. He pointed to White Fang. "Look at him! He's not snarling at us. He's looking at the rifle. He knows the rifle."

The dog musher threw down his rifle. "You're right, he's too intelligent to kill."

CHAPTER 12

A Bond Grows

The next day, Scott walked outside the cabin and sat down several feet away from White Fang. His hand was bandaged. White Fang bristled and snarled at the sight of him. He was certain he would receive a delayed beating.

White Fang didn't see a club, a whip, or a firearm. He was confused. Why was he free? Where were the chains to bind him? He decided to wait and see what would happen next.

The god remained quiet. White Fang's snarl slowly dwindled to a growl and then stopped altogether.

Then the god spoke. This caused the hair on White Fang's neck to rise. But the god didn't get up. He simply continued talking in a calm way. He spoke to White Fang as no one had done before. He talked softly and soothingly. There was a sweet gentleness in his voice.

In spite of his instincts, White Fang began to have confidence in this god. He felt, for the first time, a sense of security.

After a while, the god went back into the cabin. When he returned, White Fang was surprised that he still had no club or weapon. He sat down in the same spot and continued to speak gently as he held out a piece of meat. White Fang wouldn't move closer, for he knew these gods were smart. What if they still meant to harm him?

The man finally tossed the meat on the snow at White Fang's feet. While keeping his eyes on the god, he moved forward and smelled the meat. Nothing happened. He ate the meat. Still nothing happened.

The god then offered another piece of meat and tossed it to White Fang once again. This was repeated several times. But there came a time when the white god refused to toss it. He held it in his hand and offered it out.

The meat was good and White Fang was hungry. Slowly, he approached the man. Piece by piece, he ate the meat and nothing happened! Was the punishment just being delayed?

He licked his chops and waited. The god went on talking. In his voice was kindness. Kindness was something White Fang had never encountered.

Soon, the god's hands gently touched his head. White Fang was used to the strong force of a hand. But this time, it was different. White Fang growled a warning to let the god know he was ready to strike if the hand started to strike.

The hand lifted and lowered again and again. As the god did this, he spoke in soft whispers. White Fang was confused, for he had never known the sweet touch of man. This touch was pleasurable, especially when the man rubbed his ears.

This was the beginning of the end for White Fang. The ending of his old life full of hate. The beginning of a new life filled with love. But this love did not come in one day. It started with like, and from it love slowly developed.

White Fang liked this new god who let him remain free. This was far better than the life he had with Smith. And it was a different life than he had with Gray Beaver.

White Fang needed a god to protect, and this god was a fair and just god. So he remained. He took it upon himself to guard the property. As the dogs slept, he prowled the cabin, waiting to attack anyone who didn't belong.

It didn't take too long for White Fang's love to grow. Seeing his god each day filled him with joy. Despite knowing he loved this god, he didn't know how to show it. He knew how to show his anger and hatred. The only way to show his love was to keep his eyes on his god at all times.

White Fang grew to love his life. He left the other dogs alone and tolerated Matt because he was his god's friend. Because of his size and strength, he became the lead sled dog on the team.

In the spring, great trouble came to White Fang. Without warning, his master disappeared. White Fang waited in the snow for his return. He wouldn't work or eat. He just laid around the cabin floor, lifeless and longing for his master. Matt was so concerned, he wrote Scott a letter.

Several weeks later, White Fang sprang to his feet. His ears cocked toward the door. A moment later, the door opened and Weedon Scott walked inside.

White Fang's soft growl rose from his throat as Scott knelt down and rubbed his ears. But something was wrong. White Fang was bothered that he could not show his love. Suddenly, he thrust his head between his master's arm and body.

"Look at that!" said Matt. "That wolf really is a dog!"

With his master at his side, White Fang recovered quickly and was his old self in no time. A few nights later, Matt and Scott were awoken by a commotion outside. Matt grabbed the lantern and they ran outside.

"I think that wolf mauled someone."

Holding the lamp high, they found a man lying in the snow. His arms were folded across his face and throat. He was trying to shield himself from White Fang's teeth.

Scott pulled White Fang off of the man. Although snarling and growling, White Fang stood still and did not disobey his master.

Matt helped the man to his feet. It was Beauty Smith! Next to his feet were a chain and a club. He had come to steal White Fang!

Without another word, Scott turned Smith around and pushed him in the direction from which he came. It was the last they ever saw of that coward.

Journey on a Steamer

Something was in the air. White Fang sensed change was coming. Although he rarely went inside the cabin, he knew something was happening inside. He had heard the noises.

"Listen to that," said Matt one night. "That's one sad wolf."

Scott listened. Through the door came a low, anxious whine, like a sobbing.

"I do believe the wolf's onto you. He senses you're leaving," said Matt. "He's already mourning his loss."

"I can't take a wolf to California," said Scott. "Simple as that. He'd kill the dogs on sight. He'd bankrupt me with lawsuits. In the end, they would take him away from me." He looked out the window and searched for White Fang's shadow. "It wouldn't be fair to him."

Soon after, the fateful day came when White Fang saw the bag next to the open door. His master was shoving something into it. His god, he knew, was preparing for another trip. He was going to be left behind once more!

That night, he let out the long wolf-howl. He pointed his muzzle to the cold stars and told them of his woe. He had never felt such sorrow.

Inside the cabin, the men were getting ready for bed.

"He's not eating again," said Matt. "Won't eat a bite of meat. He won't make it this time. He loves you too much to have you leave him. He's gonna die."

Scott pulled the blankets around his head. "Shut up! Do you think I want to leave him? I don't have a choice."

Neither Scott nor White Fang slept that night.

The next day, two Indians arrived to take the bags down to the steamer on the Yukon River with Matt. White Fang didn't follow, for he knew his master was still inside the cabin.

When Matt returned, Scott came to the door and looked at White Fang. He rubbed his ears and spoke lovingly. "This is it. The time to say good-bye. I must travel to a land where you cannot follow. Give me a growl so I can be on my way."

White Fang refused to growl. Instead, after a searching look, he burrowed his head out of sight between his master's arm and body.

"There she blows," cried Matt. From the Yukon rose the hoarse bellowing of a river steamboat. "Finish your good-byes. You got to get moving."

Scott knew that White Fang wouldn't allow him to pass. So while Matt distracted him, he snuck out the back door.

A minute later, Matt rushed out the front and locked the door behind him. From inside, a low whining and sobbing could be heard.

"Take good care of him, Matt. Write me often and let me know how he's getting along."

Matt turned toward the cabin. "Listen to that, will you?" White Fang was howling the way dogs do when their masters lie dead. "He'll never make it without you here."

The *Aurora*'s decks were packed with failed gold seekers. Near the gangplank, Scott and Matt shook hands as Matt prepared to go to shore. But Matt's hand went limp. He gazed past Scott and fixated on something behind him. Scott turned to see. Sitting on the deck several feet away was White Fang.

Scott smiled. "Did you lock the door?"

Matt nodded. Then Scott called to White Fang. White Fang was by his master's side in a flash.

Matt rubbed White Fang's belly. "We plumb forgot about the window. He's all cut underneath."

But Scott wasn't listening. He had to think fast. A million thoughts flooded his mind.

The *Aurora's* whistle hooted one final time, announcing the departure. Men scurried down the gangplank to the shore. Matt loosened the bandana from his own neck and started to put it around White Fang's. Scott grabbed his hand.

"Good-bye, Matt. About the wolf, you needn't write. I'll be writing to you about him!"

Matt paused halfway down the gangplank and shook his head. "He'll never understand the climate."

Scott had a smile on his face as he waved one final good-bye to Matt. The gangplank was hauled in, and the *Aurora* swung out from the bank. Scott turned and bent over White Fang.

"Now growl," he said, as he smiled and rubbed White Fang's ears.

And White Fang did.

CHAPTER
14

The Southland

When White Fang stepped off of the steamer, he was in awe of his surroundings. The log cabins were replaced by tall buildings. The streets were full of dangers: wagons, carts, automobiles, horses, and monstrous cable and electric cars. They hooted and clanged through it all.

This was power. And the power responsible for it all was the man-gods. White Fang felt like a young cub once more. He was fearful and made to feel small and helpless.

He looked around and couldn't believe how many gods there were here! He needed his master more than ever to help him now. To protect him from these new sights.

White Fang's uneasy feeling didn't last long. He was led to a baggage car and chained in a corner in the midst of trunks and suitcases. It was here that White Fang was deserted by his master. Or at least he thought he was until he smelled the man's scent on the bags next to him.

An hour later, the car's door slid open. There was his master! Outside, the city was gone. Before him was a smiling countryside, streaming with sunshine. It was peaceful. A type of Wild that he could survive in.

There was a carriage waiting. A man and woman approached his master. The woman's hands reached out and clutched his master around the neck. A hostile act in the eyes of White Fang! Weedon Scott had to tear himself free of his mother's arms to calm down a raging White Fang.

"It's all right, Mother," Scott said as he held White Fang in place. "He thought you were going to harm me. He wouldn't allow it." He rubbed White Fang's ears. "He'll learn soon enough. I can promise you that."

His mother laughed. "In the meantime, I will love my son from afar when his dog is around. No more hugs."

Scott looked into White Fang's eyes. "Down with you." Immediately, White Fang rested. It was his way to obey his master.

"You can hug me now," said Scott. "He won't bother you again."

Judge Scott inched forward to embrace his son. This time, White Fang didn't react.

After everything was loaded into the carriage, they were off. White Fang ran alongside the horses and continued to snarl at them to warn them to be careful with his master.

Fifteen minutes later, the carriage arrived at the home of Judge Scott and his wife. Almost immediately, a sheepdog appeared before White Fang. White Fang's instincts told him to attack. But when he saw that the dog was a female, he knew he could not.

The sheepdog didn't know of that instinct. She only knew of the instinct to attack wolves, since they had attacked her kind since the beginning of time. As White Fang tried to approach the house, Collie blocked him. White Fang had no choice but to knock her to the ground to escape her.

The next moment, he met Dick. Dick saw White Fang as a stranger and would do anything to protect his master. Before White Fang could see this dog, Dick barreled into him and caused him to tumble over. When White Fang got up, Collie knocked him off his feet once again.

Scott rushed over to help White Fang. With one hand, he held White Fang while Judge Scott called off Collie and Dick.

"I must say, this is a pretty warm reception for a poor wolf from the Arctic," said Scott. White Fang calmed down under the caressing hand. "In all his life, he's only been known to go off his feet once, and here he's been rolled twice in thirty seconds."

It would be the last time another animal knocked him off of his feet.

CHAPTER 15

The God's Domain

White Fang quickly made himself at home at Judge Scott's place. He had no more trouble with the dogs. They obeyed their gods and must have decided that if their god allowed the beast inside, they had to accept it.

Dick was the first to accept White Fang. If he had his way, they would have become good friends. But White Fang did not want friendship. He just wanted all the dogs to leave him alone.

For a time, Dick tried to play with him, but eventually, White Fang's snarls were obeyed. Dick finally gave up and didn't pay much attention to him after a while.

Not so with Collie. While she accepted him because the gods said so, she saw no reason why she should leave him in peace.

Woven into Collie's being was the memory of countless crimes he and his kind had committed against her kind. The ravaged sheepfold would not be forgotten! She wanted to retaliate. She knew she couldn't go against the god's wishes, but she planned to make life miserable for White Fang. A feud, many ages old, was between them. She would see that she paid him back for all the ill his kind had created.

White Fang came to understand his master's family. Gray Beaver had Kloo-kooch and Mit-sah. He understood that his master had possessions as well. In this house, there were many such possessions including the master's children, Weedon and Maud.

White Fang did not like children. He hated and feared their hands. He couldn't forget the cruel taunting that came from their mouths back at camp. But Weedon and Maud were loved by his master. So, White Fang knew he must protect them.

Although it took a while, he grew to love them and welcomed their hands on his body. Although he allowed the members of the family to pet him, he never would give the special love croon to anyone but his master. He also refused to snuggle against them. That was reserved for his master and his master only.

There was much to learn outside of the master's house. He was used to the laws of the

North. In the North, all animals could be eaten. It was a matter of survival. He did not know that it was different here in the South.

Following his natural instincts, he ate a chicken that he came upon one morning. It had escaped from its coop and was an easy target. Later that day, he saw another chicken by the stables. As he was about to pounce on the animal, a stable hand came running with a whip. He lashed out at White Fang. White Fang, following his instincts, attacked the man and sunk his teeth into his arm.

Collie was watching this unfold and rushed into the yard to protect the man. Collie was relentless in her attack on White Fang. She was so fierce, she forced him to run off into some woods in the distance.

When Scott heard of the attacks, he knew he had to teach White Fang that the chickens were not his for the taking. But to teach White Fang this, he knew he'd have to catch him in the act.

Two nights later, White Fang's lesson was about to begin. He snuck into a coop that held fifty white Leghorn chickens. When Scott saw the slaughter the next morning, he called to White Fang. White Fang was unaware that there was anything wrong.

Scott spoke to White Fang in a harsh voice. This scared White Fang. Then Scott shoved White Fang's nose against the dead chickens and smacked him. He then led White Fang into a yard where chickens roamed free. As soon as White Fang was ready to pounce on one, Scott firmly commanded White Fang to stop.

When the judge heard of the story, he was angry. "You can never cure chicken-killers once they get a taste of blood."

But Scott knew his father was wrong. He devised a plan. "Father, I know White Fang. He has learned his lesson. To prove it, I'll lock him in the coop with the chickens for the afternoon. For every chicken he kills, I will pay you a gold coin. But for every ten minutes he spends inside without harming any, you must admit he's the smartest dog around. You must say, 'White Fang, you are smarter than I thought.'"

A deal was struck.

All afternoon, the family spied on White Fang to see what he would do. The very first thing he did? Take a nap! After he woke up, he walked around the pen minding his own business.

Later that evening, to Scott's delight, the judge sat rocking in a chair and told White Fang what a smart dog he was!

That was just one of many lessons that White Fang learned. He soon knew that the meat hanging from the hooks in the butcher's market was off limits to him. Attacking dogs and cats that belonged to gods was off limits, too.

He had to accept that some strangers would want to touch and pet him. When they did, he learned that he wasn't allowed to snap at them or show his teeth.

One day, he passed a saloon where three dogs rushed up to attack him. They had done this several times in the past, at the encouragement of their owners. This time, Scott lost his patience. He stopped the carriage and spoke to White Fang. "Go get them, old fellow."

White Fang was surprised! He had been tame for too long. Scott repeated his orders. "Go get them! Eat them up!"

White Fang jumped out of the wagon and attacked the dogs. Within minutes, two of the dogs lay dead. The third ran off whimpering.

That was the last day any dogs attacked White Fang. Word spread about the Fighting Wolf, and all the gods knew it was wise to leave him alone.

CHAPTER 16

The Reward of a Hero

The months came and went. White Fang was happier than he had ever been. And yet, he remained somehow different from other dogs. The Wild still lingered in him, and the wolf merely slept.

He never played with other dogs. Lonely he had lived, and as far as the other dogs were concerned, he would remain that way.

All the dogs looked upon him with suspicion. He aroused their instinctive fear of the Wild. Therefore, they always greeted him with a growl. He ignored them and no longer bothered to show his teeth at them or return the growls.

But there was still one annoyance in White Fang's life—Collie. Despite Scott's efforts to coax her into a friendship with White Fang, she refused. She had never forgiven him for the chicken coop incident. Since that day, she became a pest to him.

Anytime White Fang was near an animal on the farm, Collie would yap and force him away. He grew tired of her ways and tried his best to ignore her. His favorite way of ignoring her was to lie down and pretend to sleep.

One of White Fang's duties was to accompany his master as he went out on horseback. He loved this time to run free beside his master.

One day, a jackrabbit darted out in front of the horse's feet. The horse stumbled and Scott sailed through the air. When he landed on the ground, his leg was broken. Although he tried to get up, Scott could not get back home.

"Home!" said Scott to White Fang. "Go home and get help."

White Fang didn't want to leave his master.

"It will be okay," said Scott. "You must go home and get help. Tell them what happened."

White Fang knew the meaning of home. He just didn't understand the rest of the message. He turned and trotted away reluctantly. Then he stopped and stared back over his shoulder. He didn't want to abandon his master.

"Go home," cried a sharp voice.

This time, White Fang obeyed. When he arrived home, the family was on the porch taking in the cool afternoon.

"Looks like Weedon is home," said Judge Scott. He scanned the yard before him for a sign of his son.

The children welcomed White Fang back with cries of delight. White Fang growled at them. He flashed his fangs. This frightened everyone.

"He's making me nervous," said their mother. She stood up but quickly sat down as White Fang approached her. He started to nudge her to her feet and bit the corner of her skirt.

"A wolf will always be a wolf," said Judge Scott. But he didn't finish his thoughts.

The growling became fiercer. White Fang seized the woman's dress and started to drag her until the fabric tore away.

Then the judge spoke. "I believe he's trying to speak. Something is wrong!'

At once, they were all on their feet, following White Fang. He led them through the woods to where his master lay.

White Fang became a hero that day.

Even Collie seemed to sense he was a hero. She became playful with White Fang. He soon forgot how she had made such trouble for him in the past.

One day, she led him off on a long chase into the woods. White Fang knew he was supposed to accompany his master as he rode that day. But his instincts overcame him, and he felt compelled to go with Collie.

They played and romped in the woods throughout the day. By evening, they lay side by side and thought about the children that would be theirs someday.

CHAPTER 17

The Sleeping Wolf

It was about this time that a man, Jim Hall, made a daring escape from San Quentin Prison. He was a terrible man. He was in jail for murder. During his escape, he killed three guards and took their weapons.

The newspapers had many stories about Hall. A reward was offered for his capture. Men promised to hunt him down.

At Sierra Vista, the fear was real. For Judge Scott was the one who had sentenced Hall to fifty years in prison for the murder.

When Hall heard the verdict, he vowed to one day seek his revenge on Judge Scott and his family. Although Judge Scott wasn't afraid, his wife was very much so.

White Fang knew nothing of this. However, he did know that a secret was born between the judge's wife and himself. Each night, after everyone had gone to bed, she arose and led White Fang into the house.

Now, White Fang was not a house dog and was never permitted to sleep inside. But with the news of the daring escape, Alice thought it best to let White Fang sleep in the hall. Before the sun rose, she would once again go downstairs and lead White Fang back outside.

On one such night, while everyone slept, White Fang awoke. He smelled a strange god's presence. His ears heard the strange god's movements. White Fang followed the man. He had learned the advantage of a surprise attack long ago.

The strange god paused at the foot of the great staircase. White Fang knew that everything his master loved was up that staircase. As the stranger's foot started to rise, White Fang attacked.

He gave no warning. Into the air he jumped. He lifted the stranger's body and forced him to land on his back. He buried his fangs in the man's neck.

Sierra Vista awoke in alarm to the sound of shots. It sounded like a battle was raging on downstairs. But almost as quickly as it started, the fighting stopped. The struggle had not lasted more than three minutes. Everyone gathered at the top of the staircase.

Weedon Scott pressed a button and the staircase and hallway flooded with light. Judge Scott and Weedon cautiously descended the steps. Carefully, they turned the body over to reveal the stranger's face! It was Jim Hall!

White Fang had protected his family. Hall was dead. But, White Fang was near death himself.

"I don't think he'll make it," said the doctor that was called to help. "He has three bullet wounds, a broken leg, and three broken ribs. He has one chance in a thousand to make it." Then he gently rubbed White Fang's head. "More like one chance in ten thousand."

"Never mind the expense," said Judge Scott. "He saved my life and now I must save his."

White Fang had come straight from the Wild. He was strong. A survivor. With the love and help of the family, White Fang was nursed back to health. It was a miracle!

The day came when the last bandage was removed from White Fang.

"He must learn to walk again," said the doctor. "Now is as good a time as ever. Take him outside."

And outside he went, like a king, with all of Sierra Vista about him and tending to his every need. He was so weak when he reached the lawn, he had to rest.

After a while, he was able to get back up and inch forward toward the stables. In the doorway, he saw Collie with six pudgy puppies playing about her in the sun.

White Fang looked at them with a wondering eye. A puppy romped forward and looked at White Fang. Their noses touched. White Fang felt the warm tongue of the puppy on his chin.

White Fang licked the puppy back. The other puppies came forward to meet their father. They tumbled over him and nipped as his nose.

White Fang closed his eyes and soaked up the healing sun and the loving family that surrounded him.